USBORNE HOTSHOTS
CROSSWORD PUZZLES

Corinne Stockley

Designed by Isaac Quaye

Crosswords supplied by Probyn Puzzles

Series designer: Ruth Russell

*Illustrated by: Andrew Beckett, Gary Bines,
Trevor Boyer, Andy Burton, David Cuzik,
Peter Dennis, Ian Jackson, Steven Kirk, Chris Lyon,
Martin Newton, Louise Nixon, Michael Roffe,
Chris Shields, Annabel Spenceley, Guy Smith,
Sue Stitt, Stuart Trotter, Phil Weare, Sean Wilkinson,
David Wright and Norman Young*

You and your body

Across

3. Your hands are at the ends of them. (4)
5. The framework of bones your body is built on. (8)
7. Little round things you may take to make you better. (5)
8. You bend it when you jump or curtsy. (4)
10. People have two (ants have six, spiders have eight...). (4)
11. Covered in enamel and used for biting! (5)
14. A common childhood illness. (7)
16. He looks after your 11 across. (7)
18. A very common winter illness you might catch. (4)
20. If other people can catch it, you have an .... (9)
21. The state of your body. Are you in good .....? (6)

Down

1. It covers your body. (4)
2. A group of sports which keep you fit - they may be track or field. (9)
3. Where your foot joins your leg. (5)
4. The proper word for your backbone. (5)
6. Your 10 across might be put in this if you break them! (7)
9. The organs of sight. (4)
12. A dance-based form of 13 down, sometimes using steps. (8).
13. To keep fit with regular activity. (8)
15. A type of 13 down in the water. (8)
17. You breathe with them. (5)
19. The mixture of food you eat - you should have a healthy one. (4)

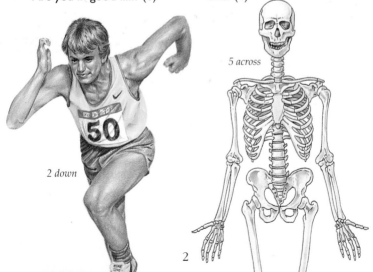

2 down

5 across

2

17 down

19 down

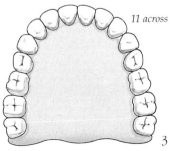

11 across

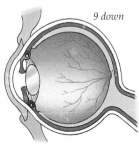

9 down

3

The world of plants

Across

3. A prickly desert plant. (6)
5. You might kiss under some at Christmas! (9)
6. A fertile place, with water and plants, in a desert. (5)
8. The green parts of a plant where all its food is made. (6)
10. A prickly evergreen - a Christmas symbol. (5)
11. A common forest tree - sounds like a sandy seaside place. (5)
12. A "thorn" of a 3 across. (5)
15. A common wild plant with a yellow flower. (9)
18. A tree - its leaf is the emblem of Canada. (5)
19. The normally brightest part of a plant which holds its pollen. (6)
20. What a tree's trunk is made of, or a place full of trees. (4)
21. Its leaves have three parts. If you find one with four - you're lucky! (6)

Down

1. One of the seasons, when very little grows. (6)
2. Part of a garden, where you grow a mixture of plants. (9)
3. An evergreen tree with very fragrant wood. (5)
4. A prickly plant - the emblem of Scotland. (7)
7. A climbing plant - a symbol of Christmas. (3)
9. Pollution which falls from the sky and damages trees. (4,4)
13. Part of a 19 across. (5)
14. Grapes grow on it. (4)
16. A plant whose leaves can give you a nasty sting. (6)
17. The part which contains a new young plant. (4)

20 across

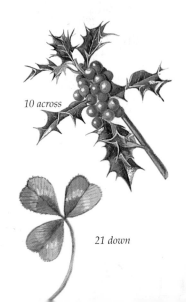

10 across

21 down

4

5 across

19 across

3 across

3 down

15 across

5

Seas and oceans

Across

1. A large, hunting fish - not always as vicious as the movies make out! (5)
5. The main ocean food - millions of microscopic creatures. (8)
6. A bright coral reef fish. Does it have a halo and harp? (5,4)
9. A sea creature, like a tortoise, with a shell and flippers. (6)
11. One of the main oceans of the world. (8)
14. A boat which takes passengers across a strip of water. (5)
16. A dark, long-necked sea bird, often seen on cliffs. (9)
19. A boat used to rescue people in distress at sea. (8)
20. An intelligent, beautiful marine mammal. (7)
21. Surging waves reaching the shore, or to ride on them! (4)

Down

1. A large group of fish. (5)
2. Tiny animals, eaten by the ton by many whales. (5)
3. A sailing boat. (5)
4. A type of shellfish which is good to eat. (6)
7. A loud, common seabird. (4)
8. Another word for salt water. (5)
10. A sea creature with five "arms" with suckers on. (8)
11. One of the main oceans of the world. (6)
12. A small boat, which you paddle. (5)
13. A type of shellfish, which may hide a pearl in its shell. (6)
15. A flat, basic boat - used to escape from a desert island? (4)
17. A border, where the land meets the sea. (5)
18. A floating anchorage point or marker. (4)

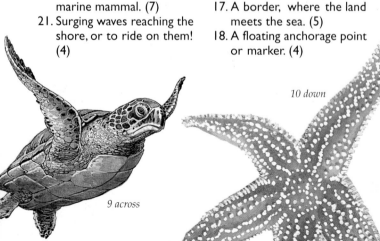

10 down

9 across

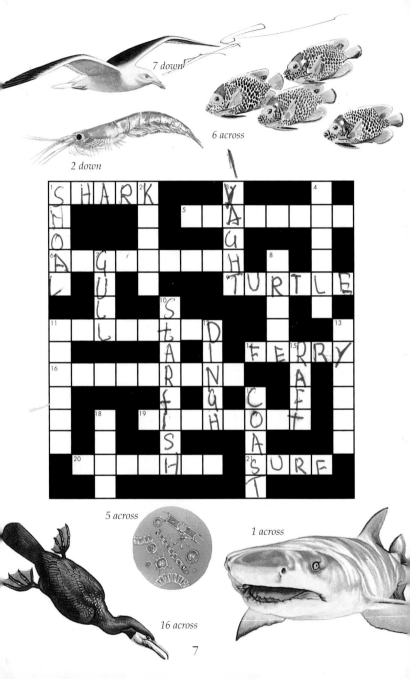

7 down

6 across

2 down

S	H	A	R	K					Y					4		
							5		A							
S	N	O	A	L					U							
									G		8					
6 O		G	U	L				9	H	T	U	R	T	L	E	
A		U					10	S								
11 L		L				12	D				14 F	E	R	R	Y
							I				R				13
16							N				A					
			18		19		G		17 C	O	A	T			
							H				S					
20						21	S	U	R	F						

5 across

1 across

16 across

7

Making music

Across

3. Trumpets and trombones belong to the .... family of instruments. (5)
5. A percussion instrument you bang and shake. (10)
6. Two performers are a .... , and so is whatever they sing or play. (4)
7. A lightweight brass instrument often played in brass bands. (6)
9. A large stringed instrument an angel may pluck! (4)
11. Many stringed instruments are played using one of these. (3)
12. The main instrument of Scottish 17 across. (8)
13. Different musical sounds or tones - and the marks used to write them down. (5)
15. A classical musical play, with singers such as sopranos and tenors. (5)
17. The traditional music of a country or region. (4)
19. Spanish flamenco dancers often click these in their hands. (9)
20. A famous Austrian classical composer. (6)
21. Percussion instruments you bang. There are many types, such as tom toms. (5)

Down

1. A stringed instrument held like a guitar, used to play some North American 17 across. (5)
2. An air-filled box you squeeze in and out to make musical sounds. (10)
3. A famous German classical composer. (9)
4. The wind instrument many people think of when you say jazz. (9)
8. A type of music which started in Jamaica. Bob Marley is famous for it. (6)
10. Music may be recorded on a .... tape. (8)
14. A wind instrument found in every orchestra. (4)
16. The main keyboard instrument, used in many different types of music. (5)
18. There are black ones and white ones on a 16 down. (4)

9 across

4 down

15 across

1 down

20 across

21 across

16 down

14 down

9

Technology and machines

Across

3. A flying machine with a rotor, not wings. (10)
6. A small truck, perhaps for local deliveries. (3)
7. The family vehicle. (3)
8. It takes people or satellites into space. (6)
9. The American word for the British "lift" that takes you up or down between floors. (8)
13. You take photographs with it. (6)
15. A farm vehicle which pulls loads or tools. (7)
17. The box you watch cartoons or shows on. (10)

Down

1. Do you have a personal one at home (a PC)? (8)
2. A flying machine. (5)
4. A moving set of steps which takes you up or down. (9)
5. A machine that can do jobs a person would do. (5)
10. It runs on rails (track) and carries people or goods. (5)
11. A two-wheeler with pedals. (7)
12. A narrow, intense beam of light used, for instance, to cut things. (5)
14. A 7 across has one, to make it move. (6)
16. Do you listen to music on it? (5)

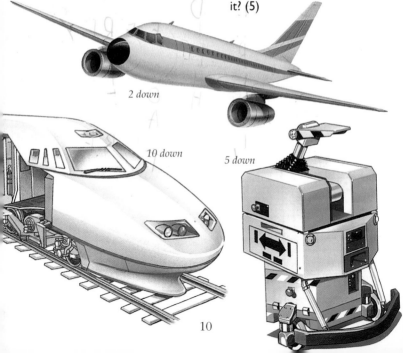

2 down

10 down

5 down

17 across

15 across

14 down

7 across

8 across

Desert and grassland animals

Across

4. A desert animal with a hump (or two)! (5)
5. A shaggy North American prairie animal, which once roamed in huge herds. (5)
7. A large, flightless Australian relative of the 12 across. (3)
9. The desert grasshopper. In a 13 down, it can cause great damage to plants. (6)
10. It eats insects (so its name says) using a long sticky tongue. (8)
12. An African flightless bird - the biggest in the world! (7)
14. African 2 downs have much bigger ones than their Indian relatives. (4)
16. A word for a tropical grassland, where a 12 or 19 across might live. (7)
17. A large, flightless South American relative of the 12 across. (4)
19. A very long-necked African leaf-eater. (7)
20. A desert relative of the spider - with pincers and a sting in the tail! (8)

Down

1. The large monkey of the African grasslands. It lives in a family troop. (6)
2. A very large African grassland animal with a very long nose! (8)
3. A North American type of wolf - often called a prairie wolf. (6)
5. A common cagebird - naturally wild in Australia. (10)
6. A snake with a well-known warning noise! (11)
8. One of the two extra-long teeth of a 2 down! (4)
11. A small African mongoose, which lives in very well-organized family groups. (7)
13. A huge gathering of insects. (5)
15. A type of South American grassland. (6)
18. An African meat-eater - the king of the beasts. (4)

6 down

10 across

12

1 down

5 down

9 across

7 across

3 down   17 across

13

Planet Earth

Across

3. Winter and spring are two of them. (7)
5. A high peak of land, sometimes with snow on it. (8)
6. The Atlantic is one. (5)
8. It goes with 10 down. (7)
9. A man-made waterway. (5)
11. It's thicker than mist. (3)
13. When the sea reaches farthest up the beach. (4,4)
14. What you study when you learn about the Earth. (9)
15. Water on grass and leaves early in the morning. (3)
17. The proper word for when rocks get worn away. (7)
19. A piece of land surrounded by water. (6)
20. Frozen water - there's lots at the 1 down! (3)
21. The gas we need to breathe - it's in the air. (6)

Down

1. The southernmost point of the Earth. (5,4)
2. A low place between hills. (6)
3. Frozen water falling from the sky. (4)
4. A "finger" of stone hanging down, often in a cave. (10)
7. A black fuel is brought up from one. (3,4)
10. A bright flash in a storm. (9)
12. A dense area full of trees. (6)
16. A hurricane is a very strong one. (4)
18. You are one of the human ....! (4)

5 across

7 down

1 down

10 down

15 across

3 down

12 down

15

Ancient worlds

Across

6. A place of government, where Roman senators met. (6)
7. Where ancient Romans washed, and spent their leisure time. (5)
9. The people of an ancient South American civilization. (6)
10. An Egyptian goddess, sister and wife of Osiris. (4)
11. The most important city of ancient Greece, and the capital today. (6)
12. The most important city of ancient .... ! (4)
15. The king of all the Norse gods, and the god of battle. (4)
17. Huge stone tombs for Egyptian pharaohs. (8)
19. A two-wheeled horse-drawn cart in ancient Rome (often raced). (7)
21. The large fighting units of the Roman army. (7)
22. A robe worn by a Roman citizen. (4)

Down

1. In Greek legend, a monster with snakes instead of hair, killed by Perseus. (6)
2. The longest modern Olympic race, named after an ancient Greek battle victory reported by a heroic runner. (8)
3. The ancient Roman god of the sea. (7)
4. Julius .... was a famous Roman leader. (6)
5. The ruler of all the Greek gods. (4)
8. A Roman coin, worth a quarter of a denarius. (10)
13. A hero of Greek legend, whose adventures are told in Homer's famous work, the *Odyssey*. (8)
14. The country of a great ancient civilization - and the 17 across. (5)
16. An object thrown in ancient Greek games, and the modern Olympics. (6)
18. A country house in ancient Rome. (5)
20. A city of Greek legend, besieged and finally defeated by a trick horse. (4)

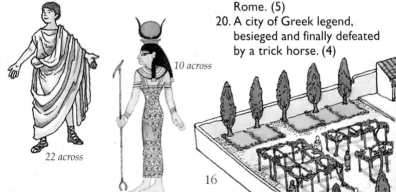

10 across

22 across

16

3 down

4 down

8 down

18 down

15 across

17

Sporting life

Across

4. It is thrown in a 15 down event. (6)
5. A forward player in soccer, who tries to score goals. (7)
7. Gliding on snow with slim boards on your feet! (6)
8. A sprinter pushes off against these at the start. (6)
11. The last defender in soccer or netball. (10)
12. A shaped piece of wood that you row with. (3)
13. An exciting water sport. (11)
18. You might wear one of these for 13 across. (3,4)
19. The controlling straps put onto a horse's head. (6)

Down

1. To stop someone's progress, in football for example. (6)
2. The first part of a horse-riding three-day event. (8)
3. The top piece that joins the posts of a soccer goal. (8)
5. A skier in the air - deliberately! (3-6)
6. A gymnastic discipline for men. (5)
9. Two-wheeling with pedals. (7)
10. A 15 down event with a long run-up. (4,4)
14. This catches the wind in 13 across. (4)
15. "Track and ......" are two types of athletics. (5)
16. You pass this in a relay. (5)
17. A scoring touch-down in rugby. (3)

10 down

5 across

18

8 across

11 across

13 across

2 down

19

Forest and woodland animals

Across

2. A mouse-sized mammal, eating the worms and insects living in the 7 across. (5)
4. A tree-living mammal. In many forests, the grey one is now much more common than the red. (8)
6. A beaver builds one of these to make a lake. (3)
7. The ground covering of dead plant matter in a forest. (4,6)
9. Hoofed forest animals of many types, such as the red and the roe. (4)
11. A small South American hunting cat, spotted like a 7 down. (6)
12. One of a pair grown and shed each year by an adult male 9 across. (6)
14. A hanging vine in a 5 down, used by monkeys and apes to swing from tree to tree. (5)
15. A flying mammal which hunts at night. There are many in a 5 down. (3)
16. An Australian mammal with a cuddly reputation! (5)
17. A long-armed ape which swings from tree to tree. (6)

Down

1. A tree with tough leaves - the only food of a 16 across. (10)
2. A slow-moving, upside-down hanging leaf-eater. (5)
3. A small, thin woodland mammal which is a vicious hunter. (6)
5. A hot, wet tropical place, home to a huge variety of animals. (10)
7. A hunting cat, at home in trees, where it stores its kills. (7)
8. A large Southeast Asian ape which spends most of the time in trees. (9)
10. A striking-looking 5 down bird with a huge, bright beak. (6)
13. A bright 5 down bird, sometimes kept as a pet. (6)
14. A beaver's home, made of sticks and branches, with an underwater entrance. (5)
15. A large forest mammal. It may be a black one, brown one or a grizzly one! (4)

11 across

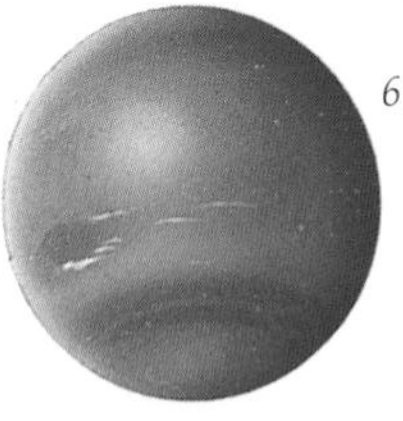

6 across

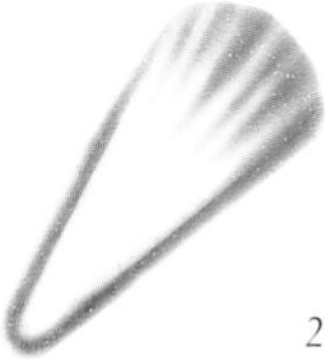

17 across

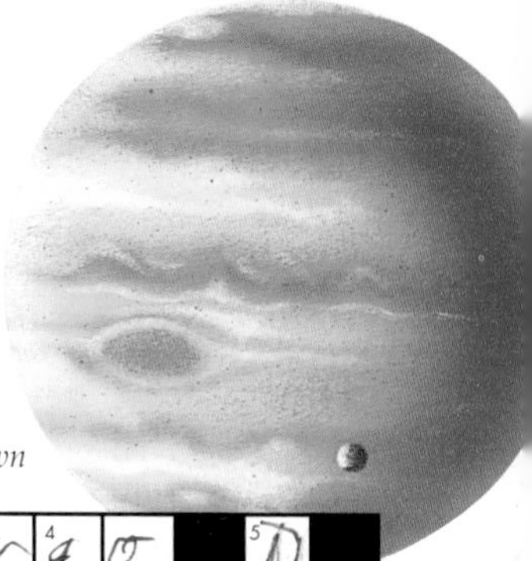

2 down

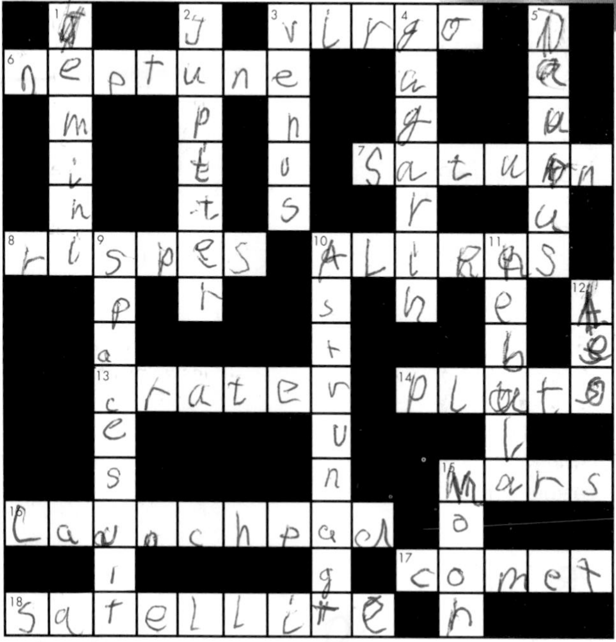

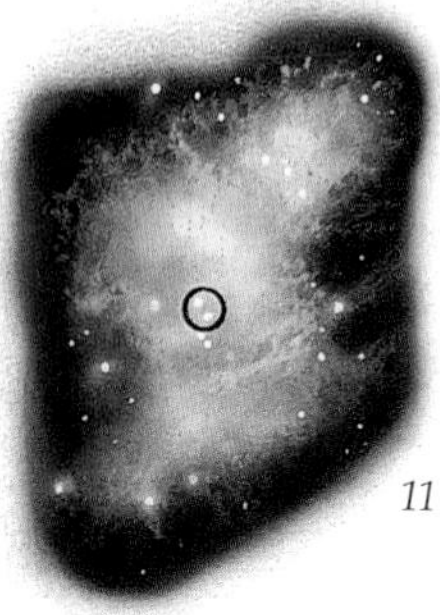

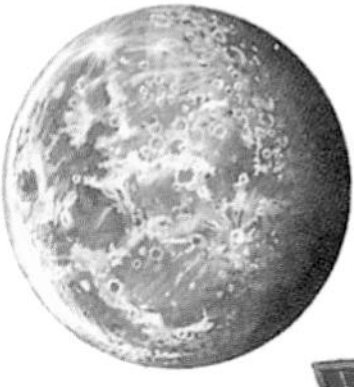

15 down

18 across

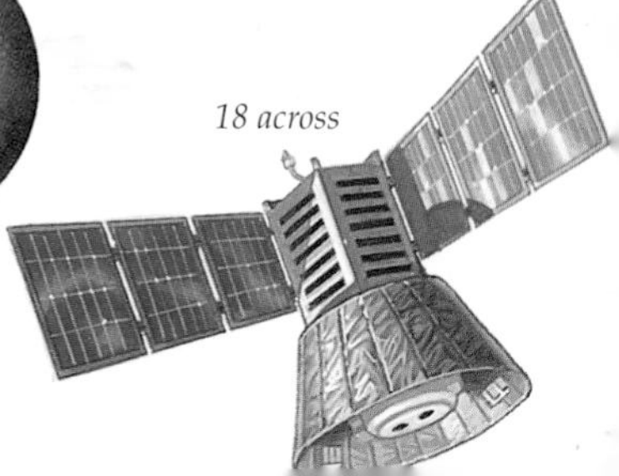

11 down

Creepy crawlies

Across

3. A hard-working insect that lives in large groups called colonies. (3)
5. A wriggler in the earth of every garden. (4)
7. A flower's sweet liquid, sipped by many insects. (6)
8. A relative of the grass-hopper, which also rubs its legs together to "sing". (7)
9. Many insects defend themselves using one of these. (5)
11. The type of 3 across that defends the colony. (7)
13. A word for snake poison. (5)
15. A common, small, green garden pest. (8)
16. A spider spins one to catch its prey. (3)
19. A garden friend with a 22 across that leaves a shiny trail. (5)
21. One of many that may live on a dog or cat. (4)
22. Many shoreline creatures live inside one. (5)
23. A 24 across may live in one. (4)
24. It collects 7 across to make honey. (3)
25. She gives birth to all the new members of a colony. (5)

Down

1. An insect with lots of legs - but not 100, more like 30! (9)
2. A snake injects 13 across into its prey with these. (5)
4. A colony-living insect that lives in a tall mound. (7)
6. A night-flying relative of the butterfly. (4)
10. A snail without a 22 across! (4)
12. It has many more legs than a 1 down. (9)
14. A flying insect that only lives for a short time - in one spring month? (6)
16. A yellow and black flying insect, much hated in summer! (4)
17. There are many types of this insect, such as a stag or dung .... (6)
18. It has pincers on its back end, and lives in dark, damp places in the garden. (6)
20. A 3 across or 16 down lives in one. (4)

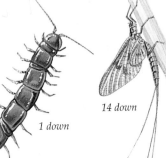

3 across

1 down

14 down

24

8 across

4 down

16 down

5 across

24 across

19 across

25

Bird world

Across

5. A bright bird, often a talking pet! (6)
6. The symbol of peace. Related to 3 down. (4)
7. A tall long-legged marsh bird - found on a building site? (5)
8. A slender sea or marsh bird. The Arctic one flies from pole to pole twice each year. (4)
10. A fish-eating hunter, related to 1 down. Rare and protected in some countries, e.g. Britain. (6)
13. A beautiful white bird, seen on many lakes and rivers. (4)
14. A female chicken. She lays eggs for us to eat. (3)
15. A slim bird which flies very fast, as its name hints! (5)
17. A small, low-nesting bird - a singer, so its name says! (7)
20. A water bird with a large pouch for fish under its beak. (7)
22. A small plump game bird (a bird shot and eaten). (5)
23. A beautiful singer - at night as well as by day. (11)

Down

1. A magnificent high-flying hunter - the king of the birds? (5)
2. A tall, long-legged marsh bird. Sometimes nests on rooftops. (5)
3. A bird often seen in towns and cities. (6)
4. A North American desert bird. It runs fast after its prey - often on roads? (10)
9. A well-known red-breasted bird. (5)
11. The very big flightless bird of the African grasslands. (7)
12. A wading bird with a long wispy crest on its head. (7)
16. A tiny bird with a short, upright tail. (4)
18. A tall, long-legged marsh bird. (5)
19. A flat-faced night hunter with large eyes. (3)
21. A loud common sea bird. (4)

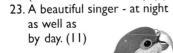

5 across

10 across

20 across

17 across

19 down

15 across

22 across

16 down

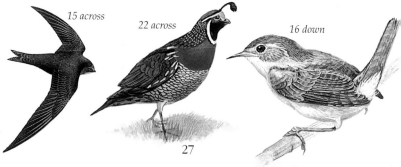

27

An A to Z crossword

Each answer begins with a different letter. There is a box at the bottom of page 29 to help you. Cross off the letters as you use them.

Across

4. The country of ancient pyramids and pharaohs. (5)
7. A spear thrown in an Olympic event. (7)
9. To sleep through winter, living on stores of fat. (9)
10. A French flan made with eggs, cheese and other ingredients. (6)
12. A type of small guitar. (7)
14. A type of animal with small gnawing teeth, such as a rat, squirrel or beaver. (6)
18. A constellation (group of stars), and a Zodiac sign. (5)
19. A type of sailing boat. (5)
20. A robe worn by a citizen of ancient Rome. (4)
23. A native Australian bird, similar to a kingfisher. (10)
25. A microscopic jumping insect - one of many that may live on a cat or dog. (4)
26. A wasp has a ....., and it may ..... you with it! (5)

Down

1. An Arctic mammal with long tusks. (6)
2. What you may take if you're ill. (8)
3. A flat stringed instrument, often played across the knees. You pluck the strings. (6)
5. A language spoken in Athens. (5)
6. The main keyboard instrument. It may be upright or grand. (5)
8. A plant whose leaves can give you a nasty sting. (6)
11. The hospital department where they can take pictures of your bones. (1-3)
13. Red-hot molten rock which streams from an erupting volcano. (4)
15. The person who prescribes your 2 down. (6)
16. A popular drink, made from crushed beans. (6)
17. A male pig. (4)
21. One of the wind instruments in an orchestra. (4)
22. A type of metal, or to smooth creases out of your clothes. (4)
24. A type of insect that lives in a colony of millions. (3)

8 down

17 down

28

23 across

3 down

21 down

1 down

7

8

9

10

11 12 13

14 15 16

17 18

19 20

21 22

23 24

25 26

6 down

24 down

20 across

| A | B | C | D | E | F | G | H | I | J | K | L | M |
| N | O | P | Q | R | S | T | U | V | W | X | Y | Z |

29

Answers